MONSTER HOUSE

D1066869

DEAR DIARY

by Orli Zuravicky

Ready-to-Read

Simon Spotlight

New York   London   Toronto   Sydney

SIMON SPOTLIGHT
An imprint of Simon & Schuster
Children's Publishing Division
1230 Avenue of the Americas, New York, New York 10020
© 2006 by Columbia Pictures Industries, Inc.
All Rights Reserved.
All rights reserved, including the right of reproduction in
whole or in part in any form.
SIMON SPOTLIGHT, READY-TO-READ, and colophon are
registered trademarks of Simon & Schuster, Inc.
Manufactured in the United States of America
First Edition
2 4 6 8 10 9 7 5 3 1
ISBN-13: 978-1-4169-1820-2
ISBN-10: 1-4169-1820-5

What an unbelievable day! Today I kissed a boy—but as usual, I'm getting ahead of myself. It started out like any other day: I woke up early, read the newspaper, and did my homework so I could spend the rest of the day on my newest project— selling candy for my school.

It was Halloween. I knew I'd make a lot of money for Westbrook Prep going door-to-door to unprepared parents.

I even got one babysitter to use her stash of emergency money to buy candy! It's all about figuring people out.

Then, as I walked toward another house,
I heard these boys yell for me to stop.
They looked kind of dorky, so at first
I was prepared to ignore them.

But then the shades on the house popped open, the pathway rose up, and the house tried to eat me! The boys grabbed me by the arms and pulled me to safety!

"What *was* that?" I asked, amazed. The
boy without the cape, DJ, seemed to know
what was going on, so I stuck around
to see what he could tell me.

I needed to call my mother,
so I went back with DJ to his house.
Normally I wouldn't spend time with guys
like them, but a house just tried to eat
me, and they had saved my life!

DJ's room was a mess, covered with all these drawings and charts. Weird! DJ's friend Chowder was on the phone with his dad, being quite rude actually.

DJ said the house was a monster that ate toys and people! I called my mom right away, but guess what? She didn't believe me! DJ said it was too much for the adult mind to take. DJ was right!

He's not so dorky after all. I should
really be more open-minded when
I meet people in the future.

DJ and I realized that in a few hours kids would be out trick-or-treating, only the trick would be on them— they were going to be the house's treat!

We had to stop it, so I called the cops. We told them about the house, but they wouldn't listen either! Adults!

We tried to tease the house so the cops could see it in action, but the Monster House was smart—too smart.

Then DJ had an idea. He took us to see Skull, the wisest man they know. They only think that because he beats everyone at this video game he is obsessed with. He's actually just a pizza delivery guy. Boys!

When we arrived, DJ and Chowder were too afraid to approach him, so I did. We didn't have any time to waste!

Skull told us the house was taken over by the soul of an owner who had died defending it, and to kill it we had to strike its source of life: its heart.

We decided that the heart must be the furnace. If we put out the fire we could stop the house. And DJ had a plan.

We filled up a vacuum with cough syrup, then dressed it like a kid so the house would eat it. The medicine would make the house sleepy, giving us time to sneak inside.

But the cops came again and ruined the plan. They called us troublemakers and loaded us into their car before we even got the dummy inside the house!

That's when the house came alive and ate the two cops!

Then it ate the police car with all of us locked inside!

DJ, who it seems is very good under pressure, told us to climb through the broken back window. We got out just in time.

We were trapped in the house, but still armed, so we decided to go find the heart and put it out.

Lucky for us, the house seemed to have fallen asleep. We were tiptoeing around when DJ disappeared!

Chowder and I ran over to the hole DJ fell through, and we fell too! We landed in the basement on a pile of toys. Luckily DJ was okay, but he discovered an old circus caravan with posters of a giant named Constance. Then DJ tripped and the whole caravan shook. That's when we found the skeleton!

We started to run, and the house went
nuts again! I was afraid it was going
to eat us, but then I spotted nature's
emergency exit, the uvula. I tickled it,
and the house spit us out on the lawn.

Suddenly the owner of the house, Mr. Nebbercracker, appeared. He shouted at us to get off his property, and then started calling the house "honey."

Once again DJ caught on first. He realized that Constance *was* the house.

Then Mr. N. told us that she was his wife—the kids in the neighborhood used to make fun of her. She died in an accident while their house was being built. Her spirit took it over, and now she eats everything that comes near her!

DJ convinced Mr. N. that he had to let
his crazy house-wife go. When he agreed
to leave, the house uprooted itself.
It was like she knew what DJ had said!
We started to run, but the house chased us,
as fast as its tree-branch arms could move.

There we were, running down the street with this house chasing us! DJ led us onto a construction site. He climbed through a hole in the fence, and we followed him.

By that time it was dark, and DJ started worrying about the kids trick-or-treating and blaming himself. I felt really bad for him.

We had to help Mr. N. fight the house! Luckily we spotted a backhoe so we got on and started the engine. We saw Mr. N. fighting with the house, and Chowder screamed, "Leave him alone!" The house was out of control!

Chowder charged at the house with the backhoe as the house hit Mr. N. He fell down and DJ ran over to him. Then the house struck the backhoe, and I went flying off of it!

Seconds later DJ nearly fell on me— with a stick of lit dynamite in his hand! I lost it! "Get rid of that!" I yelled. How many times can a person almost die in one day?

DJ told Chowder to get the house to
move under a big crane. Then DJ and I
climbed to the top of the crane. DJ planned
to throw the dynamite down the chimney,
striking the furnace.

The stunt he was about to do was very daring. I knew he was scared. I told him I believed in him, then I kissed him! I'm not quite sure what came over me, but I felt like DJ, Chowder, and I had really bonded over this Monster House, and it was only right to give DJ a proper send-off.

DJ smiled from ear to ear. Then we got down to business. He asked me to hold the dynamite while he grabbed the cable and swung out over the house. I tossed him the dynamite. He caught it and threw it down the chimney. A perfect shot!

Then the house exploded!

Later we went back to Mr. N.'s house
to dig out all of the toys it had eaten
over the years. We figured giving kids
back their toys would be a real
Halloween treat!

Aside from almost being eaten by a house, this was the best Halloween ever! I had a lot of fun with DJ and Chowder. Solving the mystery of the house and then plotting its defeat was very cool— way more exciting than selling candy!